For Anna and Sam

Copyright © 2024 by Shannon McNeill

Tundra Books, an imprint of Tundra Book Group,
a division of Penguin Random House of Canada Limited

All rights reserved. The use of any part of this publication reproduced, transmitted in any form or by any means, electronic, mechanical, photocopying, recording, or otherwise, or stored in a retrieval system, without the prior written consent of the publisher — or, in case of photocopying or other reprographic copying, a licence from the Canadian Copyright Licensing Agency — is an infringement of the copyright law.

Library and Archives Canada Cataloguing in Publication

Title: Sparkles, no sparkles / Shannon McNeill.
Names: McNeill, Shannon, 1970- author.
Identifiers: Canadiana (print) 20220460612 | Canadiana (ebook) 20220460647 | ISBN 9780735270398 (hardcover) | ISBN 9780735270404 (EPUB)
Classification: LCC PZ7.1.M425 Spa 2024 | DDC j813/.6—dc23

Published simultaneously in the United States of America by Tundra Books of Northern New York, an imprint of Tundra Book Group, a division of Penguin Random House of Canada Limited

Library of Congress Control Number: 2022948591

Edited by Samantha Swenson
Designed by Jennifer Griffiths
The artwork in this book was rendered in gouache and cut paper.
The text was set in Circular.

Printed in China

www.penguinrandomhouse.ca

1 2 3 4 5   28 27 26 25 24

 Penguin Random House
TUNDRA BOOKS

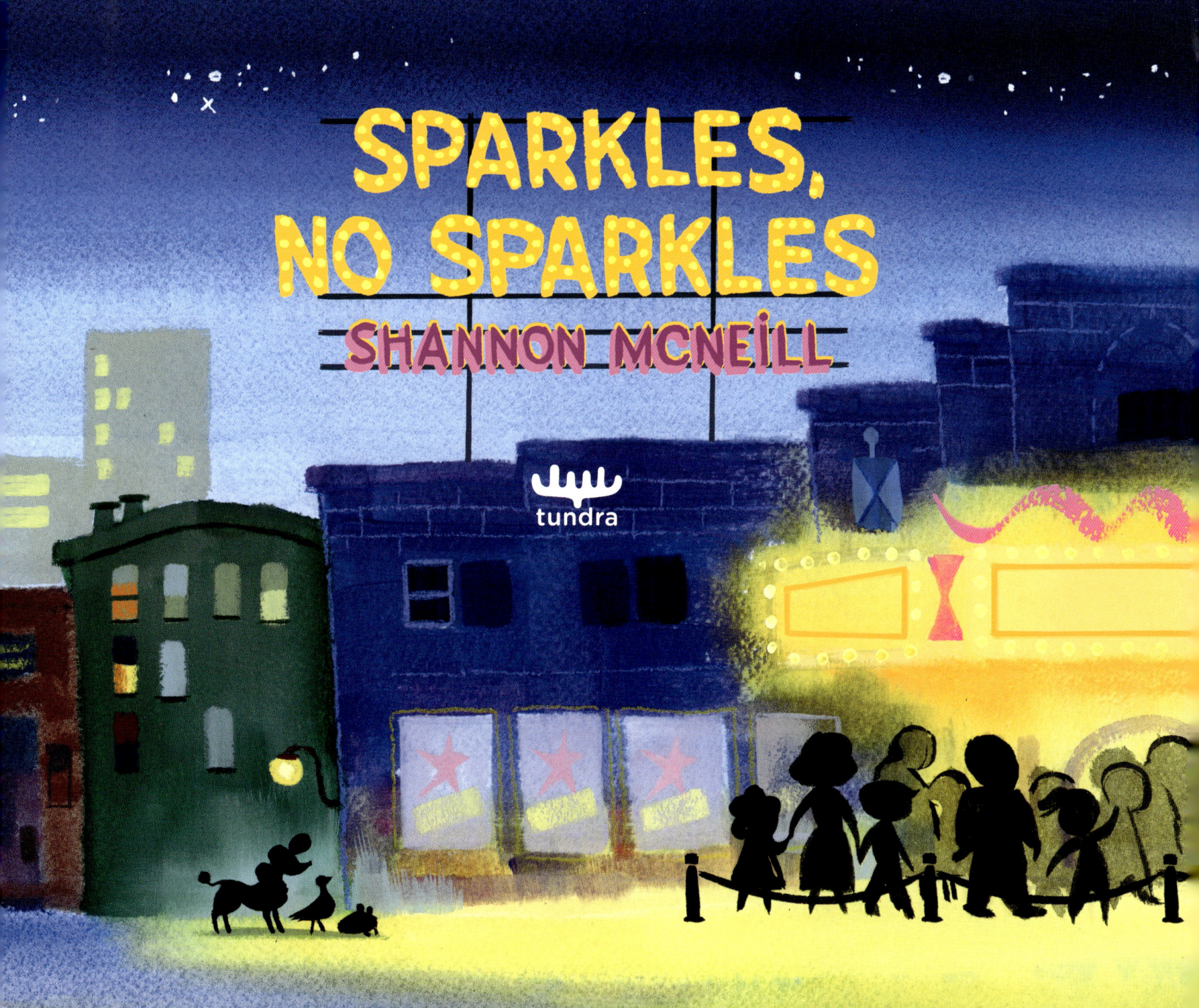

A cape has sparkles.

A toad has no sparkles.

A crown has sparkles.

A poodle has no sparkles.

Boots have sparkles.

A pigeon has no sparkles.

There is the cape.
Toad will sneak it.

There is the crown.
Poodle will snatch it.

There are the boots.
Pigeon will pluck them.

What's the deal? Animals don't steal.

For real, animals. Don't steal!

It's not for keeps! No need for warning.

We'll bring them back . . . perhaps . . . by morning.

Under the rope. Off to the show!

Toad has sparkles!

Poodle has sparkles!

Pigeon has sparkles!

Usher has sparkles?

Sadly, no.

Usher waits. It's dull and dim.
No way his boss would let him in.

Usher has no sparkles.

Here are friends that flash and startle.

Zebra and Flamingo sparkle!

All together, curtains up.

LOOK

and LOOK

and LOOK

at us!

Spinning, dipping, fringes swishing.
Someone has their wardrobe missing.

Time to exit stage right.

GOOD NIGHT!

Toad has sparkles!
Poodle has sparkles!
Pigeon has sparkles!
Usher has sparkles!
Zebra and Flamingo have sparkles!
Chicken has sparkles!